This Little Tiger book
belongs to:

_____

_____

_____

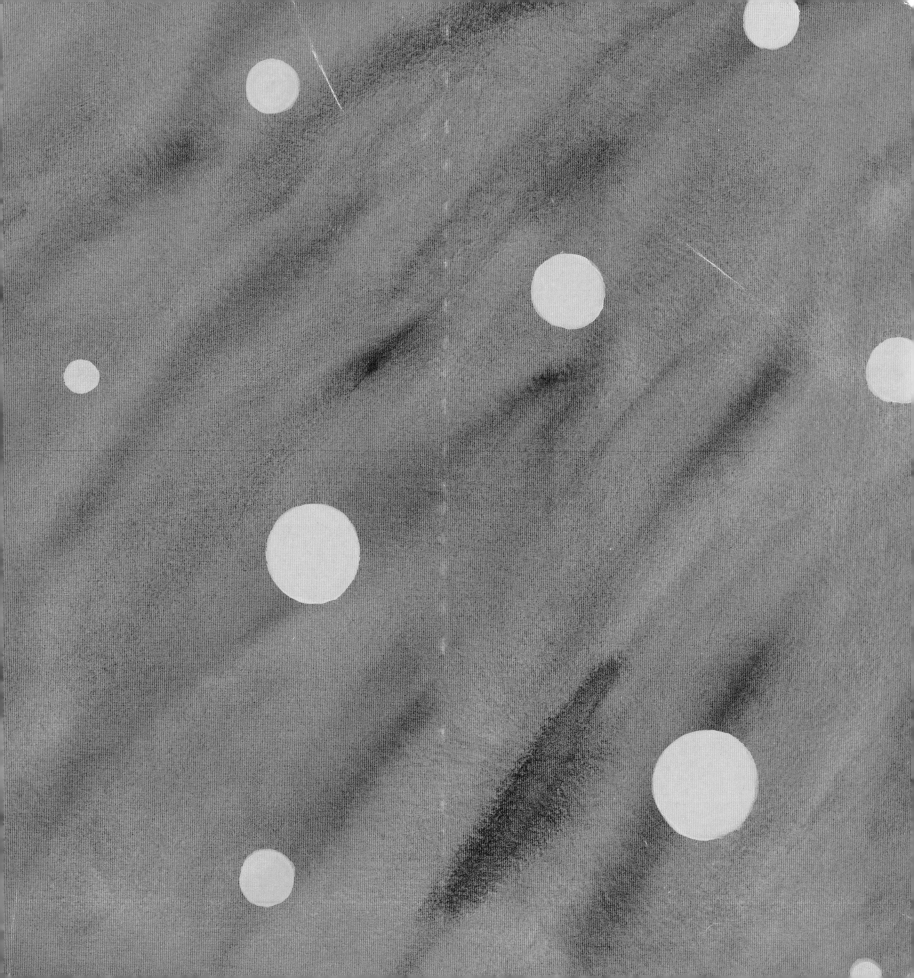

To Barney, my little shrimp – MB

LITTLE TIGER PRESS
1 The Coda Centre, 189 Munster Road, London SW6 6AW
www.littletiger.co.uk

First published in Great Britain 2014
This edition published 2014

Text and illustrations copyright © Matt Buckingham 2014

Matt Buckingham has asserted his right to
be identified as the author and illustrator of this work
under the Copyright, Designs and Patents Act, 1988

A CIP catalogue record for this book is available
from the British Library

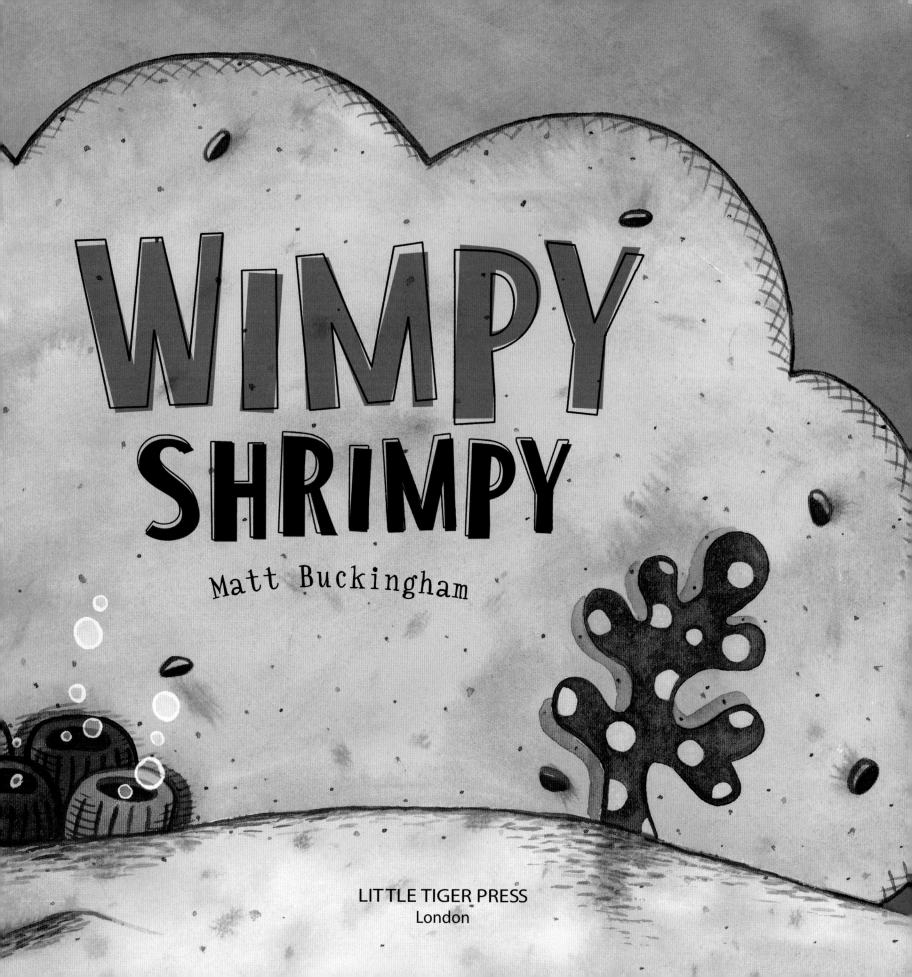

# WIMPY
## SHRIMPY

Matt Buckingham

LITTLE TIGER PRESS
London

Down at the bottom of the sea
lived a little shrimp. And this
little shrimp was a bit of a wimp.

When all his friends played happily,
Shrimpy was too scared to join in.

"Come and play hide-and-seek," called Turtle.

But Shrimpy wouldn't. He was too worried he'd get **LOST**.

"Oh, don't be **wimpy**, Shrimpy!" tutted Turtle.

"Play catch with us, Shrimpy," said Crab.

But Shrimpy thought the ball
might **SQUASH** him.
"Oh, don't be **wimpy,
Shrimpy!**" sighed Crab.

"What about hopscotch?" asked Octopus. "It's great!"
But Shrimpy was scared his legs would get **TANGLED IN A KNOT**.

"OH, **DON'T** BE WIMPY, SHRIMPY!" his friends all shouted.

"Please come and play," said Snail. "You're missing all the fun. There's really nothing to be afraid of."

In fact, Shrimpy wouldn't do **ANYTHING**. He was too worried that something bad would happen.

Then one day something **DID** happen.
Nobody asked Shrimpy to play.

Suddenly Shrimpy felt very...

. . . lonely.

Shrimpy looked at his friends all playing.
Then he began to think. Nobody was
getting lost, or squashed, or in a tangle.

Everyone was just having **FUN!**

Then Shrimpy did something **AMAZING**.
He took a deep breath and for the first
time ever he didn't worry or feel scared.
He actually began to play.
And do you know what?

He had **FUN!** His friends all cheered.
"You're **NOT** wimpy! Hooray **for Shrimpy!**"

Yippee!

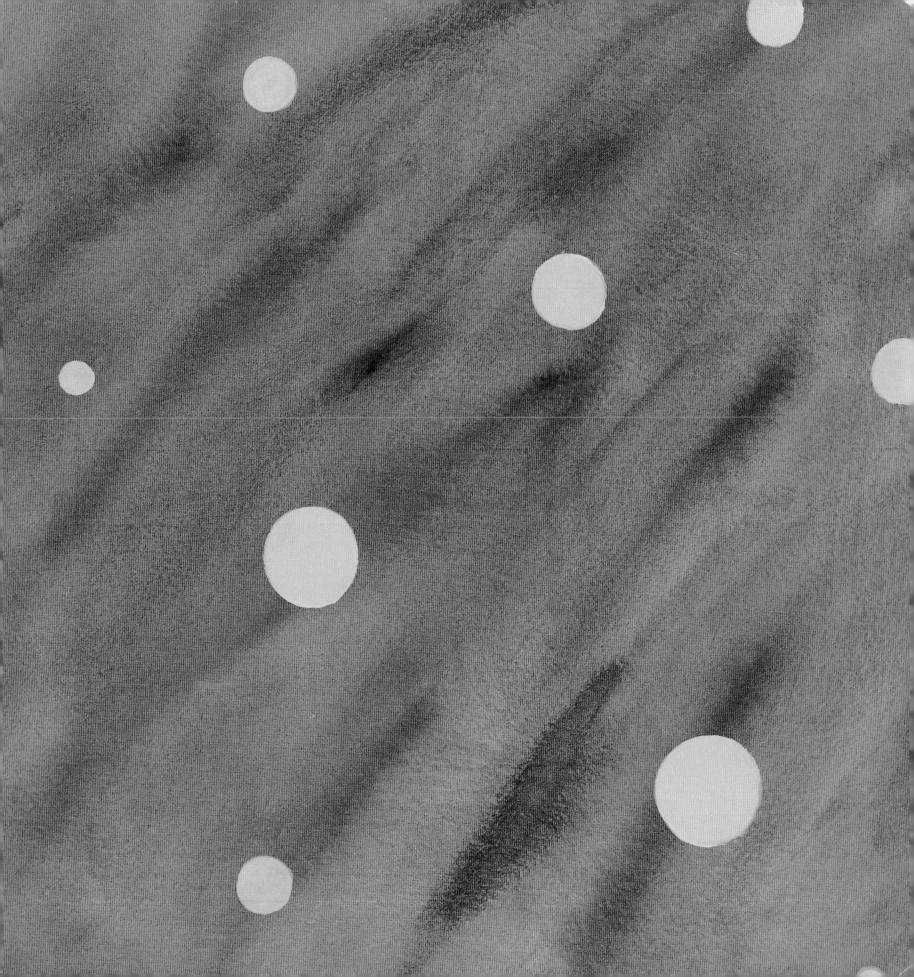

# Dive into more fabulous books from Little Tiger Press!

If You Meet A DINOSAUR
Paul Bright
Hannah George

Bright Stanley Double Trouble
Matt Buckingham

HARRY AND THE MONSTER
Sue Mongredien
Nick East

Smiley Shark and the Great BIG HICCUP!
Ruth Galloway

Eddie and DOG
Alison Brown

Abigail
Catherine Rayner

For information regarding any of the above titles
or for our catalogue, please contact us:
Little Tiger Press, 1 The Coda Centre,
189 Munster Road, London SW6 6AW
Tel: 020 7385 6333 • Fax: 020 7385 7333
E-mail: info@littletiger.co.uk • www.littletiger.co.uk